OR → Midway
11/23

KU-730-127

Please return/renew this item by the
last date shown to avoid a charge.
Books may also be renewed by phone
and Internet. May not be renewed if
required by another reader.

www.libraries.barnet.gov.uk

BARNET
LONDON BOROUGH

30131 05781723 8

LONDON BOROUGH OF BARNET

Julia
ristians

First published in the UK in 2022 by Nosy Crow Ltd
The Crow's Nest, 14 Baden Place,
Crosby Row, London SE1 1YW

Nosy Crow Eireann Ltd, 44 Orchard Grove,
Kenmare, Co Kerry V93 FY22, Ireland

www.nosycrow.com

ISBN: 978 1 83994 047 7

Nosy Crow and associated logos are trademarks and/or registered trademarks of
Nosy Crow Ltd.

Text © Ruth Quayle, 2022
Illustrations © Julia Christians, 2022

The right of Ruth Quayle and Julia Christians to be identified as
the author and illustrator respectively of this work has been asserted by them in
accordance with the Copyright, Designs and Patents Act, 1988.

All rights reserved.

This book is sold subject to the condition that it shall not, by way of trade or otherwise,
be lent, hired out or otherwise circulated in any form of binding or cover other than
that in which it is published. No part of this publication may be reproduced, stored in
a retrieval system, or transmitted in any form or by any means (electronic, mechanical,
photocopying, recording or otherwise) without the prior written permission of Nosy
Crow Ltd.

A CIP catalogue record for this book is available from the British Library.

Printed and bound in the UK by Clays Ltd, Elcograf S.p.A.

Papers used by Nosy Crow are made from wood grown in sustainable forests.
1 3 5 7 9 10 8 6 4 2

MIX
Paper from
responsible sources
FSC® C018072

www.nosycrow.com

Magnificent Mabel
and the
Very Bad Birthday

August 25th is my favourite
day of the year because it is my
birthday.

On my birthday I love
opening my presents in bed, I

love blowing out the candles on my birthday cake, and I love not having to unload the dishwasher (because when it is your birthday your parents don't force you to work).

My birthday makes me SO happy.

But there is one thing about birthdays that does not make me happy and that is . . .

. . . parties.

Like, for instance, at Harry Cox's birthday party he had a bouncy castle in the shape of a spaceship but I couldn't fly to the moon because Harry Cox and Jordi Bhogal kept landing on me.

On Florence Carter's birthday she invited everybody in Class One to feed the newborn calves at her farm but we had to take turns and the problem with taking turns is that I was always last.

At parties there are too many

people and there are also a lot of
rules.

This year I told Dad that I did
not want to have a big party for
my birthday.

"I'll just have a small one with
you and Mum and Meg," I said.

Dad looked pleased about this
and Mum said a small
party was fine with
her too. She said,

"We don't need the whole of Class One to have fun!" and then they both looked at each other and giggled.

And for once I did not mind them giggling about me because I was so glad I didn't have to have a big party. I thought, now I can enjoy my birthday without anyone ruining it. I couldn't wait.

But I HAD to wait because the

problem with having a birthday on August 25th is that it is last.

Everybody in Class One has a birthday before me.

I explained this tragic situation to my family. I said, "Why does my birthday take longer than everybody else's?"

"Mabel," said Dad. "Everybody's birthday takes the same amount of time to come around. All birthdays take a year."

"Dad," I replied, VERY patiently. "That is not the whole truth. In my class, September birthdays are first. That is what Edward Silitoe says and Edward Silitoe is a brainbox. Edward Silitoe's birthday is on September 4th."

And before Dad could argue

with me I went upstairs to my bedroom. Luckily Meg followed me up to my bedroom and even more luckily she offered to help me make a birthday countdown.

She drew lots of red boxes on a big piece of white paper and at the top she wrote MABEL'S BIRTHDAY COUNTDOWN in multicoloured letters.

"There you go, Mabel," she said. "Every morning you can cross off another box and when there are no more to cross off it will be your birthday."

I counted all the boxes. There were forty-two. It sounded like a lot but Meg said they would go very quickly.

At school, I told everybody in Class One about my birthday countdown. I said, "I thought you might need some warning so you can think of present ideas." And then, in case they didn't have any good ideas, I said, "I would quite like BIG presents if that's OK with you."

For ages I could not stop talking about my birthday. It was my favourite topic of conversation.

One day at break time I told Class One about all the things I was going to do on my birthday. I said, "I am going to dress up as a wolf and then I will put

on an amazing magic show
and afterwards there will be a
treasure hunt all over the garden
that lasts for ages."

Everybody looked really
excited, even Harry Cox and
Jordi Bhogal.

Harry Cox said, "When will we get our invitations?"

I smiled at Harry Cox and said, "Oh, I am not having a big party this year. I am just having a small birthday with my family."

Harry Cox looked fed up. He said, "If you don't invite me to your party, I won't get you a present."

I tried not to get cross with Harry Cox. I said, "Is that the whole truth?"

Harry Cox nodded. He said, "You only get presents if you have a party." He said, "That is the rule."

I did not talk about my birthday for the rest of the day. I was very quiet. I was quite worried.

On the way home from school I told Meg what Harry Cox had said. "Is he fibbing?" I asked.

But Meg shook her head. She said, "Harry Cox is right. You only get presents if you have a party."

I was so cross. When I got home I stomped into the garden to have a think. I thought, there are twenty-eight other people

in Class One and twenty-eight
presents is a lot.

When I went back inside I
tapped Mum on the shoulder.
"Mum," I said, "I have changed
my mind. I am going to have a
big party for my birthday. I am
inviting the whole of Class One."

Mum and Dad looked worried
but I did not let them change
my mind. I was firm. I said, "I

would like a big party, please."

Then I remembered to say,

"Thank you very much indeed",

because my parents do not

usually let me have things if I

forget to say thank you.

And it worked. Mum and Dad
agreed that I could have a big
party if I really wanted one.

After that I felt much better.
Meg helped me write the

invitations and I handed them out to everyone in Class One.

For the rest of my birthday countdown I was very busy getting things ready for my big

party. I practised magic tricks
for my show and I told Mum to
make the treasure hunt REALLY
tricky. Me and Dad made a wolf
suit that had grey and white
ears and a stick-on nose. I was so
excited.

Finally it was August 25th.
On my birthday morning
I had presents in bed and
pancakes for breakfast and

after I had finished opening
all my presents I didn't feel fed
up because I knew I still had
twenty-eight more to open.

When it was time for my party,
I got changed into my wolf
suit and smiled at my guests.
But straightaway I had to stop
smiling because Harry Cox was
wearing a wolf costume too.

Harry Cox's wolf costume had sharp teeth, a sticky-out tongue and a long tail. It was not homemade. It was very professional.

I tried telling Harry Cox that I am the one who likes wolves in Class One. I asked him if he even knew how many teeth a wolf has. But Harry Cox did not listen to me. He ran into the garden.

I explained to Mum that I would prefer to stay inside and open my presents if that was OK with her, but Mum said, "No."

She said I had invited all these people and now I had to look after them. She said I would have to wait until later to open my presents. She made me carry all twenty-eight presents up to my room and put them in a big pile next to my bed.

Then she told me to join everybody else in the garden.

When I was getting ready for

my magic show I kept a close
eye on Harry Cox's wolf. I could
tell just by looking at him that
he was not kind or pleasant. He
was quite wicked. I was a bit
worried that he might ruin my
party.

I was right.

In the middle of my magic
show, that wicked wolf ran up to
me, lifted up my red silk scarf

and pointed
to the
disappearing
coin.
During the card trick, he
told Lottie Clark that I had the
Queen of Spades up my sleeve.

He said I
wasn't a
proper
magician.

He ruined my whole entire magic show. I thought, someone needs to teach him a lesson.

I walked up to that wicked wolf and tapped him on the shoulder. Then I got out my magic wand and poked him a tiny bit hard in the tummy.

Unfortunately Mum spotted me. She was VERY cross.

I tried telling Mum that it was

not my fault a wicked wolf was
ruining my party but she would
not listen. She made me say
sorry to that wicked wolf. Then
she started doing the treasure
hunt.

Straightaway I concentrated because I really wanted to win the treasure. I worked out all the clues at toppity speed. But then I noticed that the wicked wolf was COPYING ME. He was CHEATING.

I grabbed that wicked wolf's tail and I pulled it ever so gently to stop him cheating. It was not my fault he was not a very strong wolf. It was not MY fault that he fell on to a slightly sharp piece of gravel.

35

Harry Cox took off his wolf
costume and threw it into a
flower bed. He showed everyone
a tiny graze on his knee. He said,
"Mabel Chase is MEAN" in a
loud voice.

Mum put a
plaster on Harry
Cox's graze and
then she gave HIM
the treasure. She did
not ask Harry Cox to share that
treasure with me. She asked me
to go upstairs to calm down.

I picked up Harry Cox's wolf
costume (because that is called
being helpful) and stomped

upstairs to my bedroom.

I lay on my bed and looked at the costume. It was extremely wolfish. It was just my sort of thing. I thought, I may as well try it on.

But as soon as I put on that costume something bad happened. I became VERY wicked.

I drew colourful pictures on

my duvet cover, I played with
Meg's remote-controlled dog,
I used a tiny bit of Mum's new
lipstick.

Finally I spotted my birthday
presents. I thought, it is not
MY fault I am a wicked wolf. I
opened every single one of my
presents, even though Mum
had told me to wait. That's how
wicked I was.

Then I heard Meg calling my
name.

I took off the wolf suit and
went back downstairs. I had had

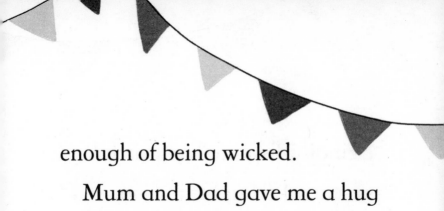

enough of being wicked.

Mum and Dad gave me a hug
and told me it was time to blow
out my candles. Everybody sang

"Happy Birthday" and when I cut the cake I made a wish, and I wished that everybody would go home. And I couldn't believe it because very soon after that my wish came true.

After I had said goodbye to everybody, I went back inside and flopped on the sofa.

"Well, Mabel," said Dad, smiling at me. "Was it a good birthday?"

I did not say anything for a long time. I was busy thinking. I remembered that I didn't have any more presents to open. I thought, that is a shame. I thought, that is not even fair.

I took a deep breath.

"No," I said. "It was not a good birthday. It was quite bad. Twenty-eight presents is not enough. Next year I am going to invite the whole school."

2

Magnificent Mabel and the Packed Lunch

When it comes to packed
lunches my parents are not
thoughtful people.

They think brown bread is
TASTY.

They are mad about CHEESE.

In Class One, everyone's
packed lunch is better than
mine.

Like, for instance, Elsa
Kavinsky has Star Bars and

teeny-tiny packets of dried mango in her lunch box.

In my packed lunch I have cheese sandwiches and a yoghurt. I have a measly apple that is hard to bite because I don't have enough front teeth.

Sometimes I think my parents are trying to starve me to death. One day when I was nibbling my apple I kept an eye on Elsa Kavinsky because she was opening her Star Bar.

The Star Bar was covered in milky chocolate. It had a crinkly red and blue wrapper.

Elsa Kavinsky took one TINY bite of her Star Bar and put it back in her lunch box. She stroked her tummy and said, "I'm SO full."

"Elsa Kavinsky," I said. "If you're not eating that Star Bar, can I have it, please?" And then

I said "thank you" to remind her
that I am a friendly person.

But Elsa Kavinsky said,
"We're not allowed to share food"
and threw the rest of her Star
Bar in the bin.

For the rest of the day
I kept thinking about that
thrown-away Star Bar.
My stomach rumbled.

In maths, when Mr Messenger
asked me tricky questions I
couldn't think of one single
answer because it is hard to
concentrate when you are
hungry and your head is full
of thrown-away food.

In literacy, I had to have a little rest because I was weak with hunger.

Except Mr Messenger did
not take my hunger seriously.
He told me to sit up and start
writing. He said, "Right now,
Mabel" in a serious voice.

That is the whole tragedy of
my life.

Luckily after literacy it
was time to watch a film.
Straightaway I started to
concentrate because the film was

REALLY interesting.

It was about a family of lions that lived in a hot and dusty place called the Great Plain. The lions were quite hungry. They were starving. They were so hungry they killed a buffalo

and ate it all up. Everyone in Class One was upset when the lions ate the buffalo, especially Lottie Clark because she wants to be a vet when she is older, but Mr Messenger explained that when wild animals are starving

they get DESPERATE and will do anything for food. Mr Messenger said that if the lions hadn't eaten the buffalo then they would have starved to death. Mr Messenger taught us about FOOD CHAINS.

For the rest of the day I could not stop thinking about those starving lions.

I was STILL thinking about

them the next day.

At lunchtime on Wednesday I only had time for a few nibbles of my cheese sandwich because I was busy keeping an eye on Elsa Kavinsky. I could not help noticing that she had left her Star Bar in her lunch box.

After lunch I decided not to go and play outside. I was weak with hunger. I lay down on a beanbag in the reading corner.

I was just like those lions.

I thought, I'd do ANYTHING to get food because I don't want to starve to death. I went to desperate measures.

When the coast was clear I walked over to Elsa Kavinsky's flamingo lunch box and opened it.

I ate her Star Bar in one gulp

(because that is how you have to eat when you are starving to death). After that I felt much better.

For the rest of the day, I was really good at concentrating. I didn't fall asleep on my desk, not even when we were practising our spellings. I put my hand up in maths. At the end of the day, Mr Messenger smiled at me and said, "Well done, Mabel, you have worked really hard this afternoon."

But on Thursday morning

I was starving again. I was
desperate.

I waited until everybody was
getting their coats for morning
break and then I opened Elsa
Kavinsky's lunch box.

I picked up her Star Bar and put it in my pocket. But when I was sneaking out of the classroom to the coat rack something bad happened. Edward Silitoe spotted me

and the thing about Edward
Silitoe is that he is a telltale.
Edward Silitoe told Mr
Messenger that I had stolen
Elsa Kavinsky's Star Bar. Mr
Messenger made me stay in at
break to have a little chat.

One thing I'm not keen on is
little chats. Little chats make
my tummy hurt.

"Mabel," said Mr Messenger.

"Did you just take a Star Bar
out of Elsa's lunch box?"

I did not answer. I did not say
one word. I nodded.

Mr Messenger looked at me,
very serious.

He said, "Taking someone
else's food is stealing."

He said, "Why did you do it?"

I took a deep breath.

"I am desperate," I explained.

"I am just like those hungry lions. I might starve to death."

Mr Messenger's eyes went all crinkly.

He said, "Oh dear" and then he cleaned his glasses. "If you're starving, Mabel, you must eat your own lunch, not Elsa Kavinsky's."

"That's the problem," I explained. "My parents only

give me cheese sandwiches and one measly apple for lunch."

(I slightly forgot to mention the yoghurt.) "Cheese sandwiches and apples are no good if you are starving. They don't fill you up."

Mr Messenger frowned.

"That's strange," he said.
"Things must have changed
since I was a child. When I was
at school, cheese sandwiches and
apples had magic powers."

I stared at Mr Messenger. "Is
that even true?" I said.

'It is one hundred per cent
true," said Mr Messenger.
"Cheese sandwiches and apples

contain magic ingredients called vitamins. Vitamins make your muscles grow. I thought everybody knew that."

I did not say one word. I looked carefully at the muscles in my arm.

Mr Messenger stopped frowning and smiled.

"When I was eight I was very small and not very strong," he

said. "So I ate cheese sandwiches and an apple EVERY DAY and do you know what? My muscles doubled in size! I ended up so strong that my teacher asked me to be captain of our class tug-of-war team."

"Oh," I said. "That is quite interesting."

I asked Mr Messenger why we didn't have a tug-of-war team

in Class One because one thing
I have always fancied doing is a
tug of war.

Mr Messenger shook his head,
sadly.

"I would love to have a tug-of-
war team," he said. "But no one
in Class One is strong enough."

"That is tragic," I said, and
Mr Messenger agreed that it
was.

I put Elsa Kavinsky's Star Bar
back in her lunch box and then
I went outside.

A bit later when it was lunch time, I ate a whole cheese sandwich and afterwards I got a ruler out of the stationery cupboard to measure my muscles. And I couldn't believe my eyes because my muscles had already GROWN!

Elsa Kavinsky sat down next to me. She said, "Mabel Chase, what are you doing with that ruler?"

"I am measuring my muscles," I said. "I have to get strong because I want to be in the class tug-of-war team."

Elsa Kavinsky said, "Oh." Then she said, "Can I be in the tug-of-war team too?"

I went a bit thinky.

"I'm not sure," I said. "Your muscles are quite small. You need to eat more magic vitamins."

Then I told Elsa Kavinsky what Mr Messenger had said about cheese sandwiches and apples.

Elsa Kavinsky looked in her lunch box.

"Mabel," she said, all whispery, "I don't have magic vitamins in my lunch but I really want to be in the tug-of-war team. Please can I have one of your cheese sandwiches to make my muscles grow?"

I looked at Elsa's muscles. I couldn't believe how tiny they were.

I took a deep breath. "OK," I said. "But if I don't eat my cheese sandwich, I will be hungry."

Straightaway Elsa opened her lunch box.

"You can have my Star Bar," she said.

I did not grab and snatch. I took Elsa Kavinsky's Star Bar very, very slowly. "Yes," I said. "That might work. I'll swap with you if you really want me to" and I handed my cheese sandwich to Elsa.

Elsa ate my cheese sandwich and I ate her Star Bar and

afterwards I measured her muscles. "The vitamin magic is working already," I said. "They are definitely growing."

Elsa Kavinsky hugged me.

"Thank you, Mabel," she said.
"You are SUCH a kind girl."

Then she noticed my apple.

"Mabel," she said. "Does dried mango have magic vitamins?"

I shook my head. I turned my voice into a whisper so only Elsa could hear me.

"I'm afraid dried mango is no good," I explained. "Dried mango makes your muscles WEAKER."

Elsa put her dried mango back in her lunch box. "Oh," she said, and she looked quite sad.

That's when I had a good suggestion.

"Elsa Kavinsky," I said in a very kind voice. "If you are so keen on getting big muscles, you can eat my apple and I will eat your dried mango for you."

I handed Elsa Kavinsky my slightly bruised apple.

"Oh, thank you, Mabel!" she

said, and gave me her pack of dried mango.

I ripped open the packet and put a bit of dried mango in my mouth. For ages I didn't even chew because I wanted the mango taste to last as long as possible.

I thought, Elsa Kavinsky's muscles might take quite a long time to grow.

I thought, it is a good job I am here to help her.

3

Magnificent Mabel and the Holiday Job

Most people think holidays are relaxing.

Holidays are not relaxing.

Holidays are HARD WORK.

Also, holidays are unfair.

Like, for instance, when we arrived at our holiday cottage in the summer I was not allowed to relax. I had to unpack all my clothes and I had to lay the table for lunch and when we had eaten lunch I had to help with the washing-up. I tried telling my parents that on holiday you are meant to TAKE IT EASY (because that is what my teacher Mr Messenger says) but Dad laughed and Mum got the hysterics.

Sometimes life isn't even fair.
After lunch, I asked if we
could go to the beach to RELAX
but Mum, Dad and my sister
Meg spent ages sitting
in their chairs in the

garden, reading. I tried to read
too but reading is hard work
and I was already WORN OUT
from all the washing-up.

I thought, SOME people in
this family need to rest.

I lay down on the grass
to have a little nap. But as
soon as I closed my eyes I felt
something tickling my neck and
then I noticed millions of tiny

ants. They were underneath
me. Someone had to save them
from being squashed and that
someone had to be me.

Saving ants was hard work.
Every time I carried one ant

to safety another one turned
up out of nowhere. I could not
keep up with those ants. When
I had rescued approximately
987,000 of them I collapsed with
exhaustion. I waited for a kind

member of my family to bring
me a cool drink but nobody
did. That's why I had to make
moaning sounds and that's also
when I had to jump on top
of Dad.

"Are you OK, Mabel?" said Dad. I blinked slowly so he would see the big bags under my eyes but he didn't notice, even though he was wearing his glasses.

I whispered, "I am MEANT to be on holiday."

I croaked, "I need a break."

I explained to that father of mine that everybody else in my

class goes on holiday to RELAX.
I said that when Sophie Simpson
goes to a hotel in Tenerife she
spends all day splashing in the
pool with her pink flamingo.
"When Sophie Simpson is on
holiday," I said in a slightly
shouty voice, "she does not have
to wash up!"

Dad gave Mum a look over
my head that he thought I

hadn't noticed but I had because I am a noticing sort of person.

That look made me cross.

"All I do is work," I explained, all shouty. "When am I going to start relaxing?"

"But, Mabel," said Dad. "You are relaxing now."

I could not believe what I was hearing. "Rescuing ants is not RELAXING," I shouted.

"Rescuing ants is TIRING."

But those parents of mine are not interested in helping me to relax. They carried on reading their books and they didn't help me rescue ants. When I needed to get changed into my swimsuit they told ME to go and find it. That is the problem with my family. They are sometimes quite cruel.

Luckily, after ages, Mum and Dad said it was time to go to the beach.

I was pleased about this because I was almost one hundred per cent certain that there would be no jobs to do at the beach. Finally, I thought, I will be able to stop working and have a relaxing holiday.

But I was wrong. The moment

we got to the beach, I had to help unpack the bags and I had to lay out my towel without getting any sand on it and then, when I was FINALLY ready to rest, I had to put on sun cream. Putting on sun cream is not relaxing. Putting on sun cream is HARD WORK. Also, putting on sun cream makes me accidentally poke Mum in

the tummy.
Sometimes life
isn't even fair.

After that I decided to go for a
paddle in the sea to cool down.
The water was splashy and fun
and it was also quite relaxing.
I thought, this is
more like it. I'll
see if Meg wants
to join in.

But when I walked back to get Meg she was playing in the sand with a girl I didn't know. The girl had blonde curly hair and a purple swimsuit. Meg waved at me, all chirpety.

"Mabel," she said. "This is our shop. Do you want to play with us?"

I thought, I love shops and I have always wanted to have one of my own.

I walked over to them.

"This is Briony," said Meg in a really happy voice.

The girl in the purple swimsuit smiled at me and then

she spoke in a silly voice, like grown-ups sometimes do when there is a baby in the room. She said, "Hello, Mabel!" She said, "You can play shops with us but remember it is OUR shop so you have to do what WE say." Then she PATTED my arm.

I thought, what a rude girl.

I thought, I wish she would go back to her own family (because

I quite fancied playing shops with Meg ON MY OWN).

But Briony did not go back to her own family. She played shops with Meg all afternoon.

Their shop had a counter and a till and they had lots of interesting things to buy, like for instance lemonade and jewellery and lots of colourful pens and pencils.

I really wanted to help on
the till but Briony said it was
too tricky for me. She said,
"Sorry, Mabel, I don't want you
to break it." Instead she kept
making me walk down to the

sea with a leaky bucket to fill
up the lemonade cups. Filling
lemonade cups was hard work. I
needed a rest.

I lay down on my towel and
closed my eyes.

But while I was resting, Meg
and Briony went for a paddle
in the sea. I could not believe
they were leaving their shop
UNATTENDED. I was shocked.

I thought, what if burglars turn up?

I sighed, like Mum does when she has too much work on her plate. I thought, SOMEONE had better keep an eye on that shop for them. I thought, I'll do it.

I got up off my towel and went over to Meg and Briony's shop.

Straightaway I could tell

that Briony was quite an
inexperienced shopkeeper
because the lemonade was not
at the front of the shop where
customers would notice it.
That's when I had a good idea.
I decided to be helpful and move
everything around.

I stacked the lemonade in
a high pyramid at the front
of the shop. I thought, thank

goodness they have me to keep an eye on things. Then I went over to check on the till and I was really surprised because it was not tricky to use, it was EASY. But then something bad happened. The till fell on top of the lemonade pyramid. Three of the lemonade cups broke and when I went to pick them up, I accidentally trod on the counter.

Soon, everything was covered in sand.

I thought, I'll have to clear this up before Meg and Briony come back.

I thought, why do I have to do ALL the work round here?

I picked up the spade and I started to dig a new shop counter but I had completely forgotten that when we were on holiday last summer a beach pixie put a spell on our spade. And the problem with enchanted spades is that sometimes they have a mind of their own. That spade was quite naughty. It would not let me rebuild the shop. It started digging a pirate ship instead.

I kept telling the spade to behave itself but it wouldn't

listen to me. It dug a massive
pirate ship out of the sand and
then it turned itself into a pirate
captain.

The pirate captain was
VERY BAD. He STOLE all the
jewellery from Meg and Briony's
shop and then he sailed across
the stormy sea to a Caribbean
island. He made me bury
his treasure for him. It was

hard work. It was not one bit relaxing. Then he fell asleep on the Caribbean island and left me to sail home all by myself.

I arrived back just as Meg and Briony were walking up the beach towards me. They were holding hands. Meg waved but I did not wave back because I was a bit too busy putting down the anchor.

That's when Briony noticed the shop.

That is also when Briony started to shout.

"Mabel!" she said in a REALLY SCARY VOICE.

"What have you done to our shop? Where is all our jewellery? YOU HAVE RUINED EVERYTHING!"

I tried to explain about the enchanted spade and the pirate ship and the bad pirate but Briony did not believe me. She gave me a mean look. She put her arm around Meg.

I could tell that Briony was

a bad influence on that sister of mine. I closed my eyes and made a wish that she would go away. But Briony did not go away. She told Meg to start making a new shop. She would not let me join in.

Suddenly I was very hot. I was so hot that sweat started pouring out of the corners of my eyes. I went to sit with Mum.

Luckily Mum spotted the sweat in my eyes.

"Mabel," she said. "What is the matter?"

So I told her about being hot and sweaty.

I said, "In my opinion this is not much of a holiday. I am EXHAUSTED and I am not one bit relaxed."

At that point I had to stop

talking because my bottom lip got very wobbly. Luckily Mum is good at understanding wobbly lips. She said she was hot too. She asked me if I thought an ice cream might help. I told Mum that it was probably worth a try.

Me and Mum walked over to the little shop on the beach that sells ice creams. In the shop was a nice shopkeeper in a stripy apron.

"Hello," she said. "Are you enjoying your holiday?"

I said, "No", because that was the whole truth.

"Oh dear," she said. "Why not?"

So I told her about having to wash up and lay the table from morning till night. I told her about Meg and Briony not letting me help with their shop (I slightly forgot to mention the enchanted spade and the bad pirate and the buried treasure). "Holidays are meant to be relaxing," I said crossly, "But all I do is work."

The nice shopkeeper did not laugh and she did not look at Mum behind my back like most grown-ups do. She smiled. She told me her name was Marta. She said, "Do you know what? I could do with a hard worker like you to help me out this afternoon."

I looked at that shopkeeper carefully.

I said, "Is that the whole truth?"

"Yes," she said. "I don't suppose you'd like a job?"

For a while I didn't say one word because I was busy counting all the different flavours of ice cream in the shop. Then I spotted the pile of lemonade cans near the door and I couldn't help thinking that they weren't very well arranged.

"I would quite like a job," I said. "But will I be allowed to use the till?"

The nice shopkeeper called Marta handed me an apron. It was stripy just like hers.

"Oh yes," she said. "This old till is very easy to use."

I stayed in that shop all afternoon. I rearranged the

lemonade cans. I welcomed customers and when they asked for an ice cream I used the roly-poly spoon to scoop it out. Sometimes I had to eat bits of leftover ice cream so it wouldn't make a mess. When I pressed the open button on the till it made a pinging sound.

Later on Briony and Meg came in to buy an ice cream. I

waved and smiled at them but I could not stop to talk because I was emptying sprinkles into a big bowl. I was very busy. I was FRANTIC.

Briony stood in the shop and watched me.

"Mabel," she said. "We have made a new shop. Do you want to come and play with us?"

I smiled NICELY at Briony.

"Playing sounds very relaxing," I said. "But I don't have time to relax."

I pressed the button on the till and it made a loud ping.

"I am working."